A Leprechaun's
St. Patrick's Day

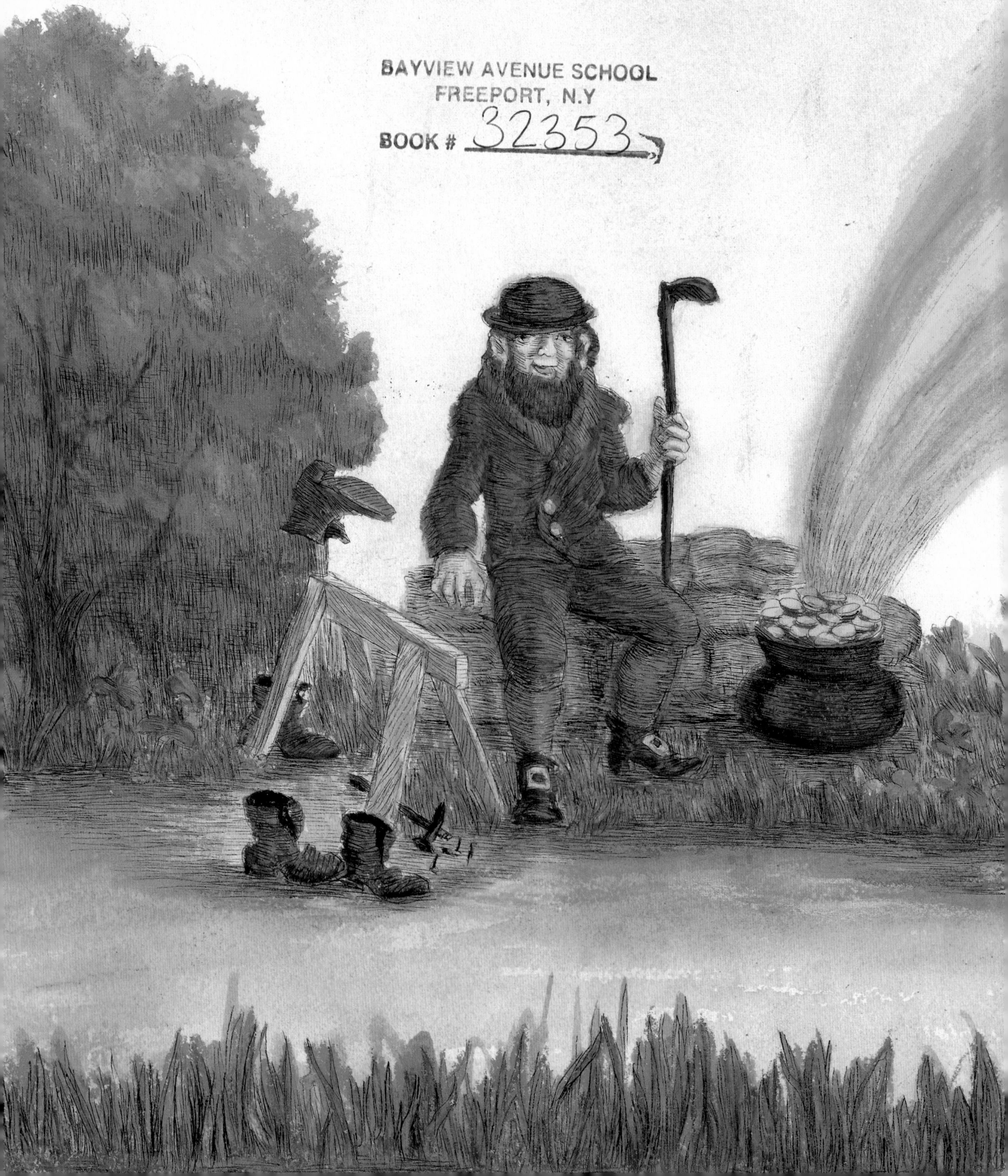

A Leprechaun's
St. Patrick's Day

By Sarah Kirwan Blazek
Illustrated by James Rice

PELICAN PUBLISHING COMPANY
Gretna 2002

First printing, January 1997
Second printing, November 1999
Third printing, September 2002

To my father-in-law, Frank, my sister-in-law, Cynthia, and my son, Beau

*With much appreciation to Dr. Milburn Calhoun and my editors,
Nina Kooij and Christine Descant*

---

*The word "Pelican" and the depiction of a pelican are trademarks of Pelican Publishing
Company, Inc., and are registered in the U.S. Patent and Trademark Office.*

Library of Congress Cataloging-in-Publication Data

Blazek, Sarah Kirwan.
    A leprechaun's St. Patrick's Day / by Sarah Kirwan Blazek ; illustrated by James Rice.
      p.   cm.
    Summary: Mischievous leprechauns plan a surprise for the St. Patrick's Day parade.
    ISBN 1-56554-237-1
    [1. Saint Patrick's Day—Fiction. 2. Leprechauns—Fiction. 3. Ireland—Fiction.
4. Stories in rhyme.] I. Rice, James, 1934-ill. II. Title.
PZ8.3.B59727Le 1997
[E]—dc20
                                                   96-22490
                                                     CIP
                                                     AC

Printed in Korea

Published by Pelican Publishing Company, Inc.
1000 Burmaster Street, Gretna, Louisiana 70053

A LEPRECHAUN'S ST. PATRICK'S DAY

'Tis a story that's told
In a magical way
Of leprechaun mischief
On St. Patrick's Day.

Eleven *"T'ank Gods"** were
Up with the dawn
Gatherin' shamrocks
On the ould Palace Lawn.

*"Thank Gods"—children

The leprechauns watched
And kept out of sight
From Ferns Castle ruins,
Where they slept that night.

Herself in the kitchen
    Makin' good breakfast bread,
    Five lovely, fresh loaves
    Coolin' out by the shed.

The leprechauns were hungry.
    "Let's go see what's cookin'.
    We'll grab a few loaves
    When herself's not lookin'."

In a flash two were gone
    As herself turned her head.
    The leprechauns feasted
    On warm soda bread.

Himself now awake,
    Down the stairs he did creep.
You know how an Irishman
    Loves a good sleep.

"*La Feile Naom Padraig!*"*
    He said with delight.

"You just put them loaves back
    Or you're in for a fight."

*"*La Feile Naom Padraig!*"—"Happy St. Patrick's Day!"

In the door flew the children
  With eleven starved faces.
  The long wooden table
  Had just enough spaces.

Herself served a feed.
  Och! What a spread.
  But himself, he was peeved—
  *Cushla** served him no bread.

*Darling or "love of my heart"

The leprechauns gathered
Out in the glade
To make their plans
For the big parade.

"Oh! Children do hurry.
    Hear the bagpipes and drums?
    Grab your shamrocks,
    Dash off to the fun."

They climbed in the cart
  Decked with shamrocks a flutter.
Ould Neddy looked back
And gave out a shudder.

Through the town, towards the church,
   From windows and trees,
   The green, white, and gold
   Waved in the breeze.

In church they welcomed
   The "Wild Geese"* home
   And prayed to St. Patrick
   That no more would roam.

*"Wild Geese"—Irish emigrants who have
   left Ireland to settle in other lands

BAYVIEW AVE SCHOOL

Then back to the cart,
  Down the ould Dublin Road,
  Through the mountains of Wicklow,
  The whole family rode

Arriving in Dublin,
  That city so fair.
  The crowds on O'Connell Street
  All stopped to stare.

The leprechauns had planned
   A peculiar switch—
   The Lord Mayor's gold coach
   Got stuck in a ditch.

The parade headed off
   As all was now ready.
   Begorra, leadin them all—
   The cart and Ould Neddy.

From the Dublin doorways
   How the crowds did shout,
   "*Slainte** to you all,"
   Raisin' cruiskeens** of stout.

The bands and the floats
   All wearin' the green,
   The loveliest sight
   You've ever seen.

**Slainte*—Good health or good cheer

**cruiskeens—small jugs

Past the grand G.P.O.*
  The parade it did wind.
  The leprechauns followed
  Closely behind.

Himself and herself,
  With their eleven T'ank Gods,
  Arrived in the stand
  'Midst smiles and nods.

*G.P.O.—General Post Office in Dublin

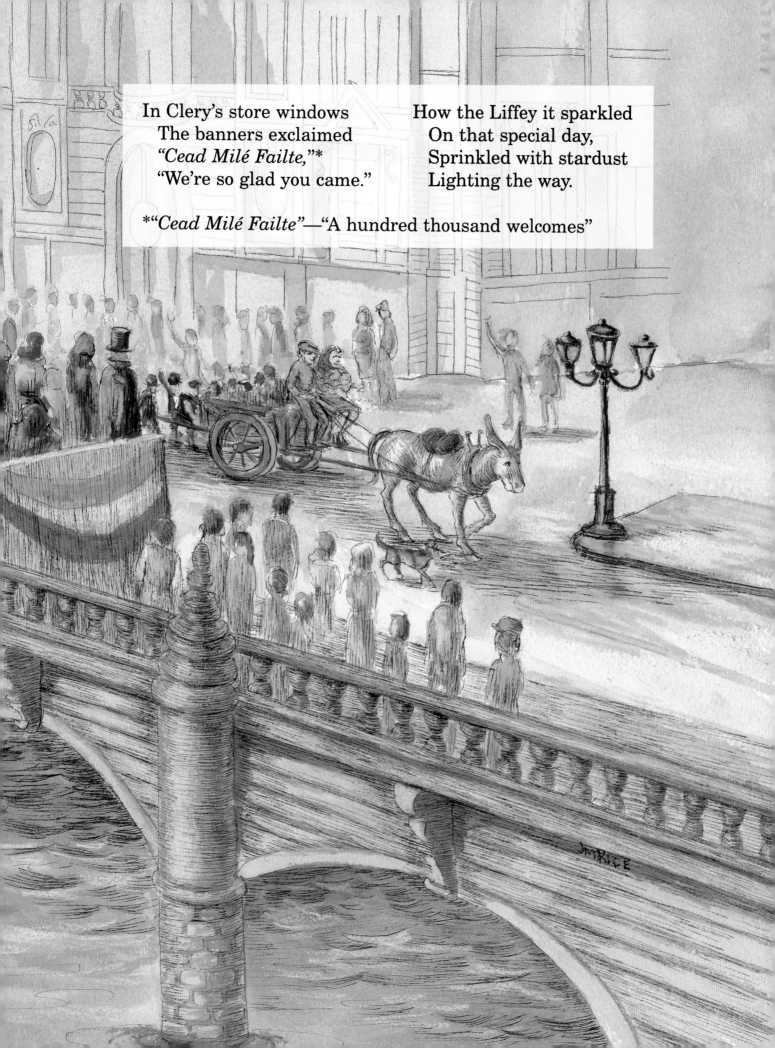

In Clery's store windows
The banners exclaimed
*"Cead Milé Failte,"**
"We're so glad you came."

How the Liffey it sparkled
On that special day,
Sprinkled with stardust
Lighting the way.

**"Cead Milé Failte*—"A hundred thousand welcomes"

Yet the day wasn't over,
For the ceili* began.
Now they jigged and reeled
To a grand Irish band.

*A large dance party.

A fine feed before them
of cabbage and bacon,
Set out for a king
And there for the takin'.

Cead Milé Failte!

St. Patrick's Day
Comes but once a year
When everyone shares
In good Irish cheer.